Toad
Weather

E Markle, Sandra

With love for Allison and Jacob Chase
and Piper Jeffery
—*Sandra Markle*

The author would like to thank Claire Morgan,
environmental educator and volunteer
coordinator at Schuylkill Center for Environmental
Education, and Dr. Doug Wechsler, director of the
Academy of Natural Sciences at Drexel University,
for sharing their enthusiasm and expertise.
Also a special thank-you to Skip Jeffery for his
support during the creative process.

I want to thank Ruby Robison and Katie Deedy
Robison over and over again. They inspired the
wonderful characters in this picture book.

Thanks as well to my mom and dad,
Ana and Thomas Sr.... Gracias!

And thanks to my wife Noni and my daughter Nina,
for also helping me with the book. Both of them
always bring me the awesome life and
happiness that I'm so privileged to be a part of.
—*Thomas Gonzalez*
August 8, 2014

Published by
PEACHTREE PUBLISHERS
1700 Chattahoochee Avenue, Atlanta, Georgia 30318-2112
www.peachtree-online.com

Text © 2015 by Sandra Markle
Illustrations © 2015 by Thomas Gonzalez

Design by Thomas Gonzalez and Loraine M. Joyner

Illustrations created in pastel, colored pencil, and airbrush on
100% rag watercolor paper. Title typeset in Bitstream Inc.'s
Geometric Slabserif 703 BT-XtraBold; text typeset in Interna-
tional Typeface Corporation's Leawood Book by Leslie Ush-
erwood, *et al.*

Printed in November 2014 by Tien Wah Press in Malaysia

10 9 8 7 6 5 4 3 2 1
First Edition

Library of Congress Cataloging-in-Publication Data

Markle, Sandra, author.
 Toad weather / by Sandra Markle; illustrations by Thomas
Gonzalez.
  pages cm
 Audience: Ages 4-8.
 ISBN 978-1-56145-818-9 (alk. paper)
 1. Toads—Juvenile literature. 2. Toads—Climatic factors—
Juvenile literature. 3. Weather—Juvenile literature.
I. Gonzalez, Thomas, 1959- illustrator. II. Title.
 QL668.E2M298 2015
 597.8'7—dc23
                              2014006505

Toad Weather

WRITTEN BY **SANDRA MARKLE**

ILLUSTRATED BY **THOMAS GONZALEZ**

PEACHTREE
ATLANTA

In the gloomy-gray
of a March day
the spring rain keeps falling.

I press my nose to the window.
But there's nothing to see outside
except the rainy-weather city.

No chance to go to the park,
ride my bike,
or play outside with my friends.
"Rainy weather makes me sad," I say.

Grandma sighs. "Me too."

Then Mama bursts into the apartment.
"Come on, Ally," she says.
"You too, Grandma.
I saw something on the way home,
something I want to show you."

"Really?" I jump up.

"What's so special that
we have to get wet?" Grandma asks.
"Besides, it's getting late."

"It's still light enough."
Mama hands us our slickers and boots.
"Come on. Get ready. Let's go."

"I think I'll stay right here,
thank you," Grandma says.

But Mama says, "Please.
Come with us."

So she does.

Out in the rainy nearly-nighttime,
streetlights are glowing.
So are shop windows.
But the world is soggy dreary.

All around us people are hurrying
        through the drizzling rain.
Cold drops slip down my neck,
so I pull my slicker hood over my head.
Then I start to hurry too,
and Grandma keeps up with me.

"Slow down, you two!" Mama says.
"There are lots of interesting things
        to see along the way."

"Like what?" Grandma asks.

"For one thing," Mama says,
"look at all the colorful umbrellas."

"It's like being inside a rainbow," I say.
"But what else is there?"

"Every rainy day is different," Mama tells me.
"You have to look around."

So I do.
I see awnings dripping.
Cardboard boxes melting.
Passing cars pushing up waves so high
that people jump back from the curb.

"But where's the surprise?" I ask.
"I vote we turn around and
go home," Grandma says.

"No. It's worth waiting for," Mama says.
"You'll see. Keep walking."

I stomp through puddles.

"Look!" Mama points at water spouting
way up high from a manhole.

"Is that the surprise?" I ask.
"Or is it all the colors swirling on the water?"

Grandma says, "Those colors are dirty old oil.
That can't be it. Is it?"

Mama shakes her head.

Then I spy an earthworm
inching across the sidewalk.
"Look at that!"

"Rainy days are perfect for earthworms," Mama says.
"Their skin has to stay wet for them to live."

While raindrops splash and splatter,
    we watch the worm crawl,
        stretching out long,
        and pulling up fat.
            Finally, the worm wiggles into a patch of grass.

        We start walking again,
            joining all the people flowing along
            the sidewalk. But now I keep an eye out
            so I don't step on any traveling earthworms.

    "What's the surprise?" Grandma asks.
    "I don't want to wait any longer."

"Listen," Mama says.
"You can hear it now."

"All I hear are raindrops drumming
on my slicker," Grandma grumbles.

"I hear people talking," I say.
"And garbage cans banging,
a dog barking,
and a crossing light beeping."

Mama says, "You hear those sounds every day.
Listen for something *unusual*."

So I squeeze my eyes tight shut and listen hard.
Then I hear it!

"It's like lots of tiny whistles," I say.
"What's making that sound?"

"That's the surprise!"
Mama takes our hands
and tugs us with her,
through the drippy, slowing-down rain,
to the end of the block.

All the while

the sound gets louder.

And louder.

And

LOUDER!

When we turn the corner,
we see lots of people,
crossing the street
and rushing back again.

A police car is blocking off the street.
Signs say TOAD DETOUR.

Other people are picking things up,
something small-as-my-palm and brown.

"My goodness!" Grandma grins.
"Toads!"

Toads are everywhere.
Crawling out of the grass.
Leaping onto the sidewalk.
Hopping across the street.

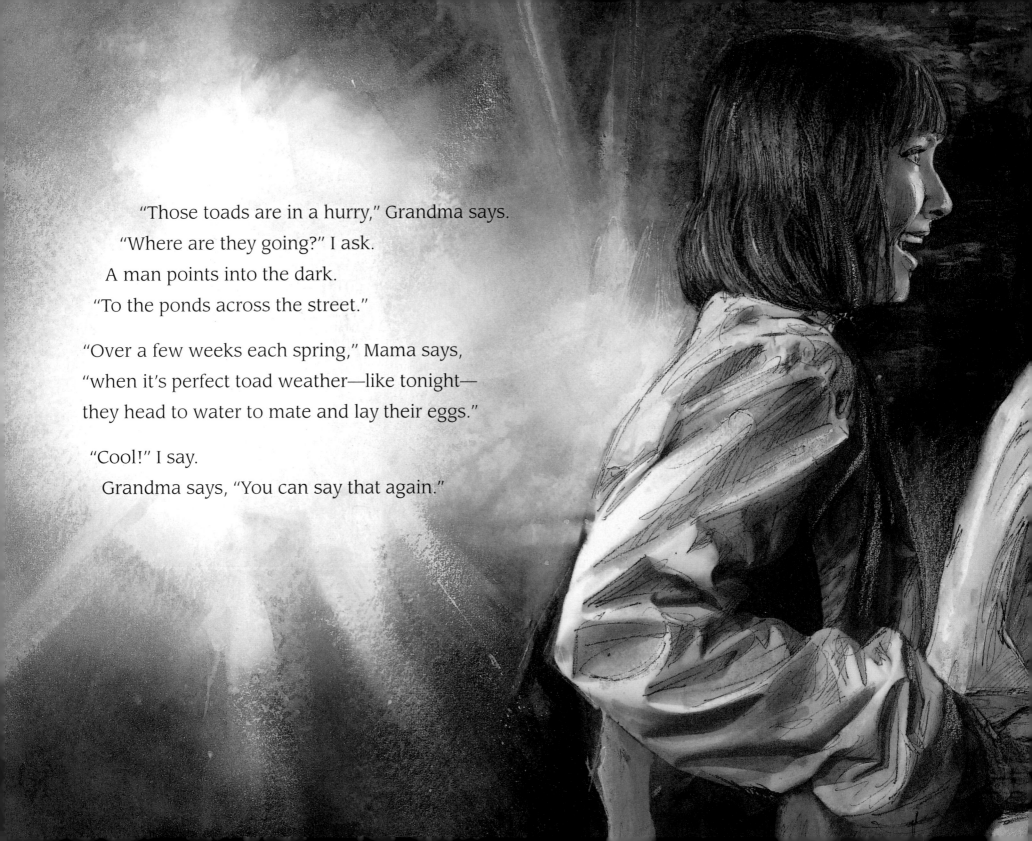

"Those toads are in a hurry," Grandma says.
"Where are they going?" I ask.
A man points into the dark.
"To the ponds across the street."

"Over a few weeks each spring," Mama says,
"when it's perfect toad weather—like tonight—
they head to water to mate and lay their eggs."

"Cool!" I say.
Grandma says, "You can say that again."

"But the toads need to cross the road safely,"
Mama says. "Do you want to help?"

"You bet!" I say.

Grandma scoops up a toad.
"Let's get to work!"

A toad hops onto the toe of my boot.
And I pick that toad up.
Bop! Bump!
The toad tries to hop out,
but I cup my other hand over it.

"Follow me," Grandma says.
So I do.

Mama passes us carrying two toads.
"Watch your step, Ally," she says.

There are toads in front of me,
beside me, and
tagging along behind me.

Tiptoeing, carefully,
I ferry my toad
across the
street.

Then I go back for another.
I make trip after trip.
Sometimes I carry two toads.
Once, I even carry three.

I don't notice when it stops raining.
But by the time the toads stop trekking,
people are leaving, and the rain is gone.

"Time to head home," Mama says.

"I admit it," Grandma says.
"That was worth going out in the rain."

"And we helped the toads," I say.
"I'm tired, dripping wet, and shivery,
but I don't care.
Toad weather makes me happy."

"Me too," Grandma says.

Grandma, Mama, and I walk home
through the dripping, freshly-washed,
after-the-toad-weather city.

AUTHOR'S NOTE

A REAL TOAD MIGRATION happens each spring in the Roxborough neighborhood of Philadelphia, Pennsylvania. The toads head to nearby ponds and the local reservoir to mate and lay their eggs.

Wildlife biologist Doug Wechsler, of the Academy of Natural Sciences of Drexel University, told me that toads trek on the first rainy night, when evening temperatures have increased to at least 50° F (10° C). The warmer weather stirs the toads from their wintertime hibernation. The wet weather keeps their skin from drying out as they migrate. While the toads don't travel in massive groups like migrating herds, Wechsler explained that hundreds of them are on the move at any one time.

Claire Morgan, volunteer coordinator at the Schuylkill Center for Environmental Education, starts preparing helpers in February. They learn about the American toad's life cycle and get tips on transporting toads. Everyone is welcome to help out—even if they haven't been through the training.

The goal of the volunteer program is to allow humans and toads to live alongside each other. After all, what are a few nights of interrupted traffic a year? For the toads, it means continuing their life cycle.

Interestingly, each year there's a second toad trek about two months later. That's when baby toads that have just changed to adult form leave the reservoir and head across the road to find a home on land.